for
aaron

Book design by Carrie Leeb, Leeb & Sons.
Typeset in Bodoni.
The illustrations in this book were rendered in casein.
Printed in China.

Library of Congress Cataloging-in-Publication Data

Knapp, Jennifer.
The go go dogs / by Jennifer Knapp.
p.   cm.
Summary: Thinking that there must be more to life, two dogs, Astro and Otto,
set off on a series of unusual adventures and find a zany English tea party, a
French circus, spaghetti trees in Italy, and more—all before dinner.
ISBN 0-8118-2028-9 (hardcover)
[1. Dogs—Fiction. 2. Voyages and travels—Fiction.] I. Title.
PZ7.K72Go   1998
[E]—dc21   98-10965
                                                    CIP
                                                    AC

Distributed in Canada by Raincoast Books
8680 Cambie Street, Vancouver, British Columbia V6P 6M9

10 9 8 7 6 5 4 3 2 1

Chronicle Books
85 Second Street, San Francisco, California 94105

www.chroniclebooks.com

the

Go Go Dogs

by

Jennifer Knapp

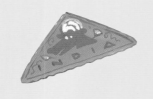

chronicle books · san francisco

This is a story about dogs. My dogs. I'm talking about **Astro** and **Otto**. Astro's head is so big he has no trouble thinking **big** thoughts. He ponders blades of grass, half empty food bowls, and **astrophysics.** That's how he got his name. With Astro so busy thinking big thoughts, our house is very quiet — *shhh!* like a library. You can hear a flea drop or Mrs. Politz next door singing to her petunias.

Then there's Otto. We found Otto hitchhiking in Kansas. When he arrived, he ate **three** bowls of dog food, **four** sausages, a **bunch** of chrysanthemums, and one old sock. Otto is usually too busy barking to waste time thinking.

exhibit A
Astro
LONG TAIL for knocking stuff over
X-LARGE
floppy ears
INTELLIGENT EXPRESSION
for finding the most rancid garbage
Otto
X-WACKY
pointy ears
NO TAIL
pointy snout for bothering the mailman
CRAZY LOOK IN HIS EYES
Beware of dogs
Mrs. Politz
exhibit B
exhibit C

The **trouble** began when Astro and Otto were paying a visit to Mrs. Politz's garbage. Mrs. Politz's garbage is known far and wide for its fruit cocktail and week old meatloaf. **Delicious!**

"Something's up and I don't like it," said Otto. "My squeak toy has lost its squeak. And Mrs. Politz's garbage has lost a bit of its zing."

"There must be more to life than this," mused Astro, chomping on the last of the really good stuff.

Otto was getting a faraway look in his eye. Astro knew this look. It meant running after cars. It meant arguing with Mr. Malvini's cat.

"Count me out," he declared.

But Otto was already digging a hole — not an ordinary, everyday hole — but a **big, humongous** hole.

"Are you coming?" he asked.

"As long as we're back in time for dinner," said Astro.

Those dogs disappeared down the hole and the rest is the story.

FAIRY TAILS

Otto and Astro surfaced in the middle of a manicured lawn. Before them stood a castle and a table **bigger** than a Rottweiler and a Great Dane put together.

"You are just in time to join us," said a gentleman wearing a tiny crown. "I'm Prince Blithering. **Welcome** to England."

Astro helped himself to one of everything. Otto dropped his fork, spilled his tea, and ate a whole platter of sticky pink sugar things.

"If you are a prince, **where is the dragon?"** asked Otto.

"Where is the wizard?" added Astro.

(Everyone knows castles come with dragons and wizards.)

"The dragon's fire went out and he retired," explained the prince. "But the wizard is around here **somewhere**."

"Here I am," squeaked Mr. Marvelous.

"**Will you do a magic trick for us?**" asked Otto.

"I'm a little out of practice," apologized Mr. Marvelous. "If you were a prince, I could turn you into a frog, but you are not. So how about an armadillo or perhaps a baboon, instead?"

"I don't think this is such a good idea," cautioned Astro. But it was too late.

"**Hocus-pocus, gobblety-gook,**" chanted the wizard. He wiggled his nose and waggled his fingers. *Poof!* One guest became a

spotted beetle, another an oyster,
and another an old, plaid couch.

"Woops! So sorry. Let me try
again," fretted Mr. Marvelous.

Poof! Suddenly, Otto's head
was on the prince's body, and the
prince's head was on Otto's. Otto
did a dance on his two new feet,
and the prince **barked** at his
guests.

Poof! All heads went back
to their proper owners, and Astro
and Otto decided it was indeed
time to go.

Back on all fours, Astro and Otto dashed into the prince's labyrinth. They ran and ran until they were right back where they had started. Astro was wishing he had brought his atlas. (If only dogs came with pockets.)

"We're lost," he said.

 Otto did the sensible thing — he put his nose to the ground and found a scent. It was all Astro could do to keep up. At last, they found

a

small

door.

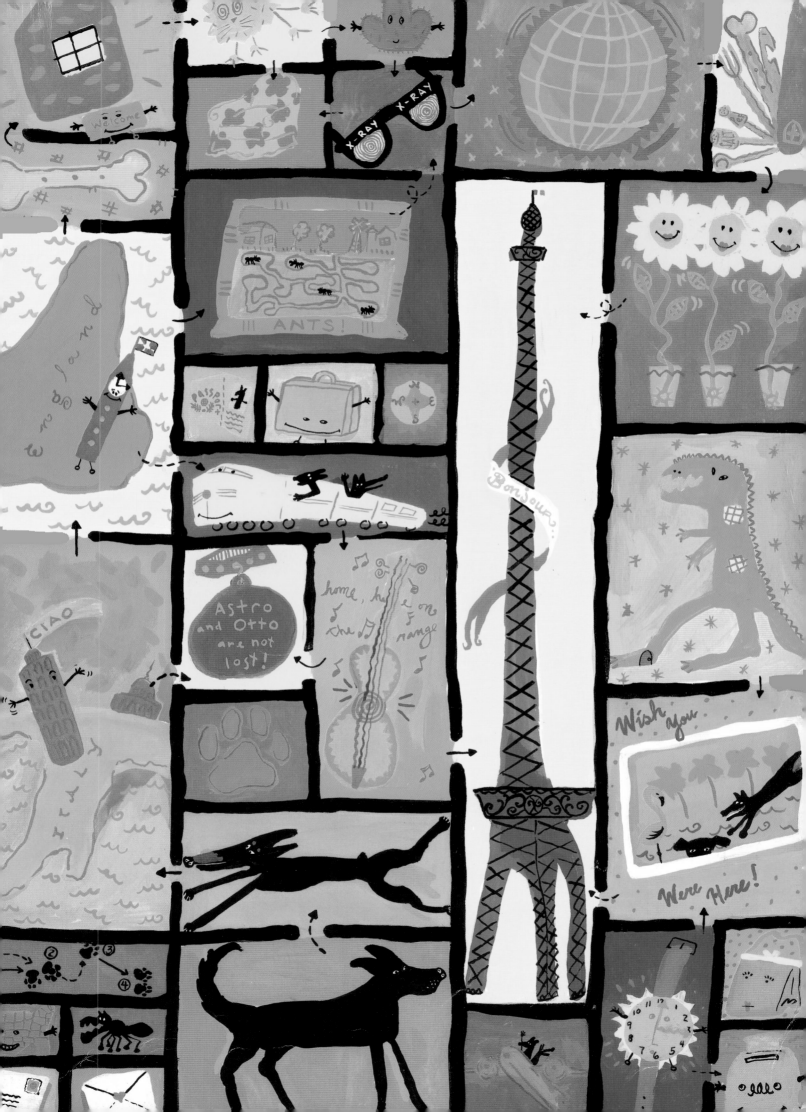

OODLES OF POODLES

Astro and Otto squished through the door and
kerplopped into a hustling-bustling plaza.
A circus troop was setting up for an afternoon
extravaganza.

"Welcome to France, mes
cheris," sang a voice from above.
"Land of eclairs and berets and
bonjour mon ami, *kiss, kiss!*"

Lulu DejaVu was tiptoeing high in the sky on a tightrope. Her tangerine hair was as tall as the Eiffel Tower. She **pirouetted** and the old men feeding pigeons *oohed*.

Before Astro could say *adieu*, Otto **leaped** up onto the tightrope, legs akimbo. He and Lulu danced the **rumba** and then the **cha cha cha**. The old men feeding pigeons *aahed*. Astro knew there were better things to do in Paris.

Just then, **Madame Mumbo Jumbo**, the palm (and occasional paw) reader, beckoned to Astro with a long, skeletal finger.

Inside her dark tent, she examined Astro's paw. **"Ooooh!"** she exhaled. The hairs in her mole wiggled excitedly. And then she spoke:

" One dog, two dogs go to France.
One dog does a **silly** dance.
You, you sit and admire towers.
When you're through you sniff the flowers.
You like to learn, you want to know.
He wants **fun**, all he does is **go.**
Though dogs you are, you will fly in the air.
And of meatballs, I say **BEWARE!**"

Astro thanked her. **"But really!** A dog warned of his favorite delicacy might as well become a cat."

Astro stepped back into the square just in time to see Otto's grand finale — a backwards, uʍop-ǝpᴉsdn flip. *Ta Dah!* The old men feeding pigeons applauded.

While Otto was busy
bowing, up walked a **bearded
lady** with a boa constrictor boa.
"You are a natural," she bellowed.

The head honcha of the big top had an
idea. Not just any idea — a show stopper.

"Ladies and Gentleman. Allow me to introduce to you,
The Whiz-Bang Flying Dog Brothers!"

The next thing those dogs knew they were being stuffed
into the mouth of a **wow-o-rama** cannon.

Now they'd *never* make it home in time for dinner.
KABAM! Off they flew. The old men feeding
pigeons gave them a standing ovation.

CIAO HOUNDS

SPLAT! Astro and Otto landed in the top of a tree. Not just any tree...

"A spaghetti tree!" yelped Otto.

"*Buon appetito!*" cried Astro.

L o n g, dangly noodles **sprouted** from the branches and **curlicued** around the leaves. The dogs couldn't eat fast enough.

"*Mama mia,*" gasped Allesandra Maria Alberpasghetti who was picking noodles for her family's spaghetti factory. "You must be from very far away. In Italy dogs do not know how to fly."

"Come with me," she said. Allesandra knew just what to do when two **big** dogs crash-landed in her spaghetti trees.

Linguini, fettucini, capellini— the first plate of spaghetti and meatballs put a wag-a-lini in Astro and Otto's tails. By seconds, they remembered their names and were polite enough to introduce themselves. And by thirds, they were all singing opera. *Spaghetissimo!*

By fourths, Astro and Otto had become so round, they rolled right off their chairs and under the table. Soon they were both snoring loudly.

Chef Al Dente

inside→

3 + ✶ =

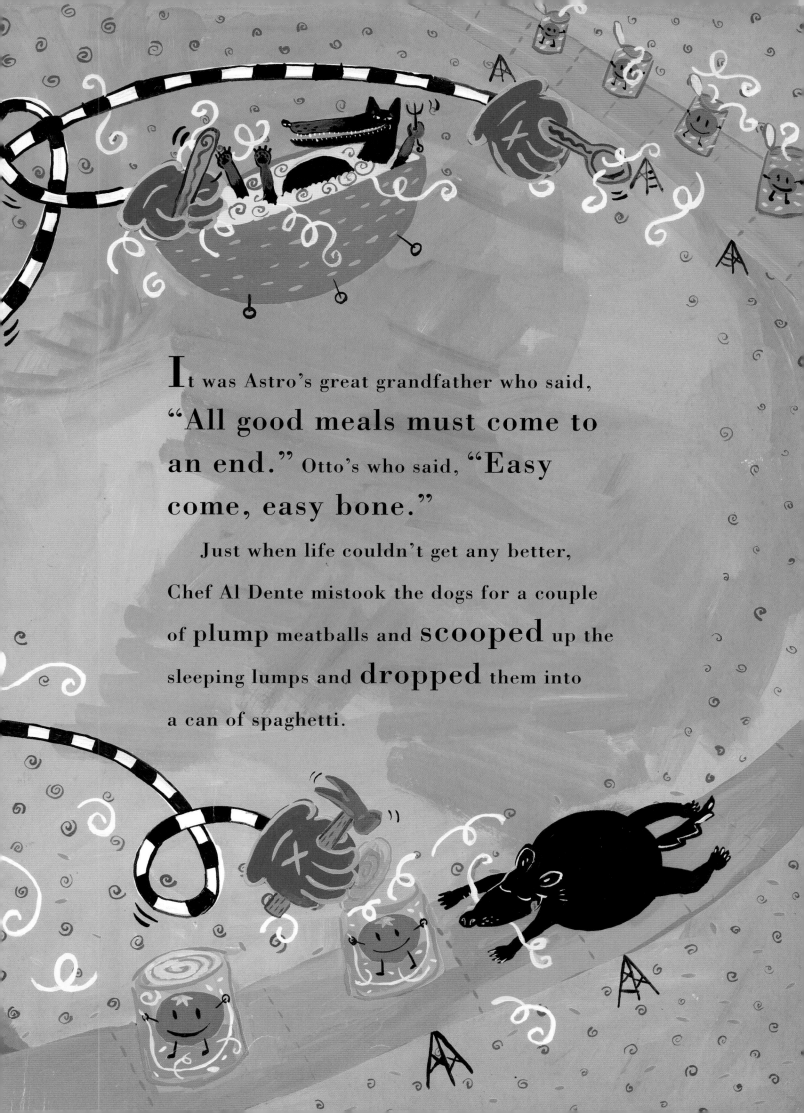

It was Astro's great grandfather who said, "All good meals must come to an end." Otto's who said, "Easy come, easy bone."

Just when life couldn't get any better, Chef Al Dente mistook the dogs for a couple of **plump** meatballs and **scooped** up the sleeping lumps and **dropped** them into a can of spaghetti.

When the can opened, Astro and Otto leaped out.

"**My meatballs have legs!**" cried the hungry raja
of Rajasthan.

The monkeys vacuuming the palace were not going to let two
perfectly good meatballs get away. They switched their vacuums
to shag and—*VROOOM!* out the door they **zoomed** into
a bustling bazaar.

DOGGIE LAMA

Astro and Otto **zigged** through an archway and **zagged** around a yak. They ran past men in candy-colored turbans and **scrambled** over baskets of **hot, hot** curries and **cool, cool** cucumbers. They joined a line of children dancing to a **twanging** sitar and wound around a belly dancer wiggling her belly bells and **jing-jangling** her bracelets.

The monkeys were not far behind.

But, in one **loony** leap, Astro and Otto were safe inside a large basket.

"I miss my bed," said Astro.

"I miss chasing Mr. Malvini's cat," said Otto.

"Stop squiggling."

"I'm **not** squiggling."

"If you're not squiggling. . ." began Astro.

". . .Who is?" finished Otto.

Hisss! It was time to go!

Astro and Otto **burst** out of the basket and landed on a heap of dusty carpets.

"Flying carpets. A very good price," smiled Ace Akhbar, used flying carpet salesman and owner of Ace Akhbar's Flying Carpets.

Astro and Otto couldn't believe their good luck.

"I see you have your eyes on this beauty," winked Mr. Akhbar, twirling his mustache. "This model comes with full shag and adjustable fringe. It is a special price today."

Otto signed an I.O.U. for everything they owned: three slobbery tennis balls, a half-eaten bone, and one squeaky, rubber pork chop without the squeak. Mr. Akhbar shook the dogs' paws and stood back as they zoomed off on their ruby red flying carpet. Luckily for everyone, Astro was driving.

Under a **saffron sliver** of a moon,
Astro turned their carpet toward home.

"We've traveled through the ground and through
the air," said Astro.

"We've been **here** and we've been **there**."

"But not there," said Otto, snout pointed toward the moon.

Otto was getting that **far away** look in his eye.

"Everyone knows the **moon** is made of **cheese**,"
said Astro, following Otto's nose.

Otto licked his lips and
Astro's stomach **growled**.

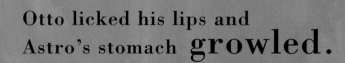

"Maybe tomorrow," said Otto.

"Because tonight we can
still make it home in time
for **dinner!**"

Those are my dogs, Astro and Otto.

Their adventure may not be over, but this story is.

Good-bye, au revoir, arrivederci, jai ram ji ki!

The End